My Animal Friends

Adapted by Erica Pass

Based on teleplays by Rosemary Contreras, Leyani Diaz, Valerie Walsh, Ligiah Villalobos, and Chris Gifford and Valerie Walsh

Reader's Digest Children's Books®

Pleasantville, New York • Montréal, Québec • Bath, United Kingdom

RAINFOREST RACE

Diego and his sister, Alicia, were at the Animal Rescue Center, getting ready for the Rainforest Race.

"Animals come from all over to be in this race," said Diego.

"The winner gets a day at the brand-new animal playground," added Alicia.

So far, there were three teams entered in the race—the Spectacled Bear Team, the Howler Monkey Team, and the Puma Team. Just then, Diego noticed a shy-looking armadillo.

"*Hola*, Armadillo," Diego said. "Are you ready for the race?"

DISK 1

"I want to be in the race," she said. "But I don't have a team."

"That's okay, Armadillo," said Diego. "I'll be on your team!"

"*¡Gracias!*" answered Armadillo. "Now I've got a team!"

FIELD JOURNAL ANIMAL FACTS
Small ball! At birth, three-banded armadillos are really tiny. They are about the size of a golf ball!

The other animals in the race were bigger than Armadillo, but they didn't have a hard shell with three bands like she did. They couldn't turn themselves into a ball like she could. And they couldn't dig as well as she could.

"Maybe our team can win!" said Armadillo.

Alicia stood in front of the teams. "There are three places you need to get through," she said. "The shaky nut trees, the muddy slide, and the giant mountain. Are you ready to start the race? Great! Ready, set, go!"

"Come on," said Diego. "Let's race!" Everybody took off running.

First, the teams had to run through the shaky nut trees. As they ran through the trees, all of the animals slowed down to cover their heads so that they would not get hit by the falling nuts. But not Armadillo—she had a strong shell to protect her.

Next, Diego and Armadillo came to a field. Diego saw a sign for maned wolves.

"Uh-oh," he said. "Armadillos are afraid of maned wolves. But armadillos can also roll themselves into balls to hide!"

(3) As soon as a maned wolf appeared, Armadillo rolled herself up until she looked just like one of the other rocks on the ground. Once the maned wolf passed, she peeked out of her shell.

FIELD JOURNAL ANIMAL FACTS
Have a ball! Three-banded armadillos have hard shells like other armadillos, but they are the only armadillos that can completely roll into a ball to protect themselves.

Next came the muddy slide, which Armadillo rolled down with no problem. After that, the four animal teams headed to the giant mountain.

Suddenly, Diego heard an animal calling for help. "¡Ayúdame!"

Diego used his Spotting Scope to see who was in trouble and saw two pumas. "It looks like one of the pumas is missing from the team," he said.

When Diego and Armadillo got there, they saw that one of the pumas was stuck inside a deep hole. He tried to climb up, but kept sliding back down.

"We need something that can help the puma out of the hole," said Diego. "Rescue Pack can help! ¡Actívate, Rescue Pack!"

With that, Rescue Pack flew off Diego's back and transformed into a rope.

"Now we need to get the rope down to the puma," said Diego. "What animal can crawl down into a hole?"

"I can do it!" Armadillo volunteered.

DISK 2
(5)

Armadillo crawled into the hole while holding onto the rope. When she reached the puma, she climbed onto his shoulder and they tied the rope around themselves.

"We're ready, Diego!" called Armadillo. "Pull us up!"

Slowly, Armadillo and the puma were pulled out of the hole.

"¡Muchas gracias, Armadillo!" said the puma. "¡Muchas gracias, Diego!"

"Now we have to keep going," said Diego. They all took off running again.

In the distance was the giant mountain.

"We're almost to the finish line!" said Armadillo.

She tried to climb up the mountain, but her legs were too short. All of the other animals were ahead of her! Armadillo's claws were digging into the mountain.

"Hey," said Diego. "Maybe there's another way for us to get to the other side of the mountain."

Armadillo used her claws to dig a tunnel through the mountain, with Diego crawling behind her.

"We made it to the other side before the bigger animals!" he shouted. "And there's the finish line. We've got to run fast! *¡Rápido!*"

FIELD JOURNAL ANIMAL FACTS
Dig it! Armadillos are great diggers. They use their strong claws and legs to dig for food. They also dig dens for themselves, where they can sleep.

All of the animals were close to the finish line. Alicia waited for the teams at the finish line. It was a very close race!

Armadillo rolled herself into a ball to gain extra speed. She raced toward the finish line. Just before she got there, she unrolled herself, and she and Diego crossed the finish line first! The other teams arrived just after.

7

"Wow, they were fast!" said the spectacled bears.

"And strong!" said the pumas.

"And smart!" said the howler monkeys.

8

Alicia handed out ribbons to everyone, but the special blue ribbons went to Armadillo and Diego, the winning team.

"As the winners of the race, you get to play at the new animal playground," Alicia told them. Armadillo looked around at the other animals and then back at Alicia. "I'd like to play at the animal playground with all my new friends," she said.

"Hooray!" cheered the animals.

"Diego," said Armadillo, "thank you for being on my team."

The animals spent the rest of the day celebrating together in their new playground. The Rainforest Race was a great success!

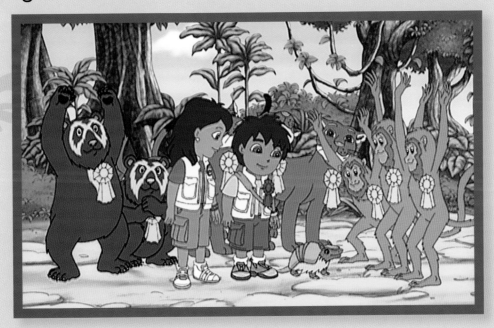

THE LITTLE LOST WOLF PUP

DISK 1

"We're Animal Rescuers!" shouted Diego.

"And I'm an explorer," shouted his cousin Dora as they zipped down the zipline at the Animal Rescue Center. Dora was visiting Diego in the rainforest.

"Dora, I've got a surprise for you," said Diego.

"I love surprises!" said Dora. "What is it?"

"Come on out!" Diego called behind him.

"Ah-ruff! Ah-ruff!" After a few seconds, a few maned wolf pups appeared.

"Wolf pups!" Dora exclaimed, as they ran toward her.

"Maned wolf pups," Diego added.

Dora hugged one of the maned wolf pups as it licked her face.

"Hi, Diego! Hi, Dora!" said Alicia, Diego's sister. She was with the mother of the baby maned wolves.

"Mommy, mommy!" said the pups as they ran to her.

"Mommy Maned Wolf came to the Animal Rescue Center to have her pups," Diego told Dora.

"She's doing great!" said Alicia. "Did you know that maned wolves can have up to five pups at a time?"

"Let's count how many are here," said Dora.

FIELD JOURNAL ANIMAL FACTS
Stand up tall! Maned wolves have very long legs, which help them to see above the tall grass. They can also rotate their large ears to listen for other animals!

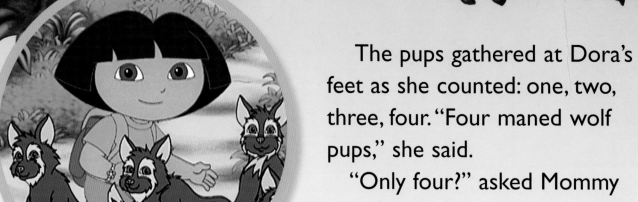

The pups gathered at Dora's feet as she counted: one, two, three, four. "Four maned wolf pups," she said.

"Only four?" asked Mommy Maned Wolf. "But I have five pups. My smallest pup is missing! And it's time for his feeding. He must be hungry!"

Diego went to comfort her. "Don't worry," he told her. "We're Animal Rescuers. We'll find your baby."

Alicia decided to stay back and help Mommy Maned Wolf and her pups, while Dora and Diego began their mission to find the missing maned wolf pup.

First, Diego asked Click, his special camera, to help discover where the pup was. Click zoomed through the forest and spotted the baby maned wolf in the middle of the prickers and thorns. He looked afraid.

③ "Oh, no!" said Diego. "The baby maned wolf is lost in the prickers and thorns!"

"And he could get hurt!" said Dora. "We need to save the baby maned wolf and bring him back to his mommy."

Dora and Diego saw three paths through the rainforest. Each had footprints, but only one set of the footprints belonged to a maned wolf. Diego used his Field Journal to decide which set of tracks to follow.

④ "Let's think like animal scientists," said Diego. "We need to find the footprints that match."

As Diego and Dora found the right footprints and followed those tracks deeper into the rainforest, they saw some other animals that were in trouble.

"Help us!" cried a pygmy marmoset family that was hanging onto a tree branch. There were three babies, a mommy, and a daddy.

"The branch is breaking!" said Dora.

"We've got to save them," said Diego.

Diego and Dora ran and jumped onto two vines, and swung through the trees toward the marmosets.

FIELD JOURNAL ANIMAL FACTS
Pygmy marmosets are the world's smallest monkeys. They spend lots of time in trees, and are often found with their family!

Diego and Dora swung underneath the pygmy marmosets just as the branch broke. The pygmy marmosets fell right into their hands!

DISK 2
(5)

"Thank you for saving us," said one of the babies.

"You're welcome," Diego said. "And now, we need to keep going so we can save the baby maned wolf, too." He used his Spotting Scope to search for more maned wolf prints.

"There they are," said Dora. "Way down the river!"

Diego activated Rescue Pack to form a raft. Dora asked Backpack to give them paddles and life jackets. But the water was very rough. As they paddled down the river, they saw a river otter stuck in a whirlpool.

"Help me throw him a life preserver," said Diego.

Diego tossed the life preserver to the river otter and with Dora's help, pulled on its rope. Together, they yanked the river otter out of the whirlpool and over to their raft.

⑥

"Thanks for rescuing me!" said the river otter.

"That's what we do!" said Diego.

"Now we've got to rescue the baby maned wolf," said Dora.

After more paddling down the river, the raft finally arrived on the shore near the prickers and thorns.

⑦

"*Ah-ruff!*" called the baby maned wolf.

"He's in those bushes," said Diego. "He sounds so scared!"

"We have to get there fast before the baby maned wolf gets hurt," said Dora.

They ran toward the maned wolf pup's sound, but they couldn't find him. Diego remembered that maned wolves have big ears and hear really well. Diego and Dora cupped their ears just like maned wolves to try to hear the baby calling.

But they still couldn't see him. Then Diego remembered that maned wolves also have very long legs, which make them tall enough to see over long grass.

"We've got to stand up tall to see over these bushes," Diego said to Dora. Finally, they saw the baby maned wolf! They ran toward him to stop him from heading into a prickly bush.

"I got lost," said the baby maned wolf.

"We know," said Diego. "But don't worry. You're safe now!"

Diego and Dora brought the baby back to his mommy and his brothers and sisters.

"I'm so happy we're back together," said the baby maned wolf, as he played with his family.

THE GREAT ROADRUNNER RACE

DISK 1

Diego was waiting in the desert for his friend, Roady Roadrunner. They were going to the Great Roadrunner Race.

"Roadrunners don't fly, but they run super, superfast," said Diego, as Roady arrived. "Roady is running in the race for the first time!"

Diego's sister, Alicia, called for Diego on his Video Watch. "The race is about to start!" she said. "Roady needs to be ready to do all the things that roadrunners do best. Roadrunners are superfast runners, but they're also great at jumping, shaking, and ducking."

"We're on our way," said Diego.

FIELD JOURNAL ANIMAL FACTS
Super speed! Roadrunners don't fly, but their strong legs can carry them quickly from danger and toward food. They can run very, very fast!

"Uh-oh, Diego," said Roady. "I don't know if I can do all those things yet. I'm not so good at jumping, shaking, or ducking."

"Don't worry, Roady," answered Diego. "We'll help you get ready."

They set out for the race. Soon, they came to a hill that led to a cactus field. Roady was running very fast, right toward the cactus field.

"¡Para!" Diego called to Roady. "Stop!"

Roady stopped just in time. "Thanks!" he said gratefully. "These cactus arms are kind of low. We won't be able to run through the cactus field."

"We will if we duck like roadrunners," said Diego. He showed Roady how to duck under one of the cactus arms. Roady followed him, and together, they made it through the field.

As Roady and Diego got closer to the starting line of the race, they passed some children on the side of the road who were cheering.

"You can do it, Roadrunner!" said a little boy and girl. They offered Diego some water and Roady some fruit.

③ "Roady's favorite," said Diego. "Roadrunners don't drink water, but they love juice from fruit."

Next, they came to some tumbleweeds rolling toward them.

"We're going to have to jump like roadrunners to get over the tumbleweeds," said Diego. "You can do it, Roady!"

Roady tried and found out that he was able to jump high over them!

Suddenly, an announcer called, "The Great Roadrunner Race is about to start. Calling all roadrunners to the starting line!"

"We've got to hurry," said Diego.

Roady took off, running fast toward a desert cave. "I can't be late!" he said. Diego watched him disappear into the cave.

"Uh-oh," said Diego, as he entered the cave. "I've got to find him. Hey, it's dark in here! I need to use my flashlight to help us see."

DISK 2

Diego listened for Roady's *coo-coo* call, and was able to find him quickly. But when they got outside the cave, they suddenly ran into a sandstorm!

"We need something to protect us," said Diego. "Rescue Pack can transform into anything we need!"

Rescue Pack to the rescue! It changed into a tent, and Roady and Diego were safe inside while the sandstorm passed. Then they started running toward the race again.

"We're almost there!" said Diego, as he and Roady approached the starting line. Suddenly, some water came down from the sky, making them slip.

"That's weird," Diego said. "It doesn't usually rain in the desert." He looked up and saw the Bobo Brothers in a hot-air balloon, spraying each other with hoses.

(6) "Help me stop those silly monkeys!" Diego cried. "Yell, 'Freeze, Bobos!'"

Roady and Diego yelled for the Bobo Brothers to freeze, and they did. The water stopped spraying down.

"Now we've got to get to the race superfast, Diego!" said Roady.

They ran as fast as they could. When they got there, Alicia was waiting. "You made it!" she said as Roady joined the other roadrunners. "Get ready to race, Roady!"

"You can do it, Roady!" said Diego.

Alicia held up a flag and said, "Ready…set…go!" And the roadrunners were off!

⑦

Besides running really fast, the roadrunners had to face three obstacles: ducking under a parachute, jumping over hurdles, and shaking through the sand. Roady was able to remember all the ducking, jumping, and shaking he had done with Diego on the way to the race, and it helped him win!

"I did it!" Roady said. "I can't believe I won! Yippee!"

"¡Felicidades, Roady Roadrunner!" another roadrunner said. "Congratulations!"

⑧

"Here's your trophy, Roady," Alicia said. "You deserve it!"

"¡Misión cumplida!" Diego said. "Mission complete!"

MACKY THE MACARONI PENGUIN

"¡Hola!" said Diego, as he headed up a mountain covered in snow. "I'm on my way to Penguin Island to meet my sister, Alicia."

Suddenly, Diego's Video Watch started beeping and Alicia showed up on the screen.

"Diego!" she said. "I made it to Penguin Island. And look—all the mommy and daddy penguins are keeping their eggs warm before they're ready to hatch!"

But there was one mommy penguin missing her egg.

"Diego," said Alicia. "You've got to find it!"

With the help of his special camera, Click, Diego was able to see the missing baby penguin. Diego changed his boots into skis and was on his way!

DISK 1

①

FIELD JOURNAL ANIMAL FACTS
Teamwork! When macaroni penguin chicks are born, the daddy penguins keep them warm while the mommy penguins go to get food each day.

As Diego got closer to the egg, he heard honking. The baby had hatched! But he still couldn't see her. He used his binoculars to find her, perched on top of a pile of snow. She was still partly in her eggshell.

"Wow, look how little she is," said Diego. "*Hola, pingüinita.*"

"*¿Mami?*" asked the penguin.

"No," said Diego. "But we're going to take you to your mommy."

Diego used his Field Journal to discover that he was holding a baby macaroni penguin.

"I think I'll call her Macky," he said.

"Honk, honk!" said Macky.

27

Diego held Macky in his palm as he called Alicia and Mommy Macaroni Penguin. "Alicia, we found the baby macaroni penguin," he said. "We're on our way!"

Diego placed Macky on the ground, but she was a little unsteady.

"I need to show Baby Macky how to waddle," said Diego. "Macky, you have to stand up and rock from side to side."

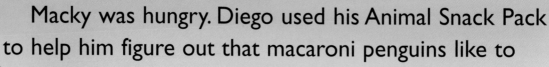

With Diego's help, Macky learned how to waddle!

"Diego," said Macky a moment later. "*Tengo hambre.*"

Macky was hungry. Diego used his Animal Snack Pack to help him figure out that macaroni penguins like to eat squid. He fed some to Macky.

"Yum!" said Macky.

In order to get to Penguin Island, Diego and Macky had to go down a mountain. But Macky looked scared.

"Macky doesn't know how to get down the mountain," said Diego. "Let's check my Field Journal to see how macaroni penguins get down tall, snowy mountains."

DISK 2

Diego discovered that macaroni penguins slide down mountains on their tummies, so that's what he and Macky did!

They were getting very close to Penguin Island. Just then, the Bobo Brothers started throwing snowballs. Macky was so excited that she didn't see the monkeys.

"We need to stop the Bobos before they hit Baby Macky with a snowball!" said Diego. "Freeze, Bobos!"

That did the trick!

Diego and Macky continued on their way—they were close! They could see the mommy and daddy macaroni penguins just across the water.

"Let's call out to them so they know we're almost there!" he told Macky. They honked and flapped their arms so the penguins saw them.

"Now we need something that will help us fly down to Penguin Island," said Diego.

Rescue Pack turned into a hang glider for Diego and Macky to use to carry them across the ocean.

"We made it to Penguin Island!" said Diego when they landed.

"Look, there's your mommy, Baby Macky!" said Diego.

Mommy Macaroni Penguin and Macky waddled toward each other and hugged.

"I was so worried," said Mommy Macaroni Penguin. "*Gracias*, Diego."

"Diego," said Alicia, "the penguin eggs are about to hatch!"

 Diego, Alicia, Macky, and Macky's mommy watched as all the baby eggs hatched. Baby Macky was especially excited because she knew she had a lot to teach the new babies—thanks to Diego.

DIEGO SAVES THE HUMPBACK WHALE

DISK 1

One day in the rainforest, Diego was looking for his friend Baby Jaguar. He asked his Papi if he had seen him.

"Sorry, Diego," said Papi. "I've been up in the mountains with Aldo the Hawk."

"Aldo," Diego asked, "have you seen Baby Jaguar?"

"He's down by the river," said Aldo.

Diego knew his Mami was also by the river. He decided to go and see her.

"See you later!" said Papi.

(2) Diego's Mami was an Animal Scientist, just like Papi. When Diego got to the river, she was helping a little caiman who had an eye infection.

"*Hola,* Diego," Mami said. "I've been out on the river making a rescue."

Mami did not know where Baby Jaguar was, either. "I hope he's not in trouble," she said.

(3) Just then, Diego heard something. "*Mreow!* Help!" Baby Jaguar called. Baby Jaguar was hanging from a loose tree branch!

"I'm coming, Baby Jaguar!" called Diego. He swooped in on a vine and caught his friend just as he began to fall.

"Thanks for catching me," said Baby Jaguar. Then Diego heard another sound: "*Aoo Ahh! Aoo Ahh!*" Another animal was in trouble!

4

With his special camera Click, Diego could see that a baby whale needed help. He was stuck on a rocky island in the ocean and had lost his family.

"I've got to save the baby humpback whale and bring him back to his mommy!" said Diego. He began to run through the rainforest, but there were lots of vines in the way.

"I know!" said Diego. "If we bend our backs, we can duck under the vines! Humpback whales bend their backs when they dive underwater, too!"

DISK 2

5

Some of the vines had spiders and snakes on them, so it was hard to get by. But Diego bent his back and made it under all the vines.

FIELD JOURNAL ANIMAL FACTS
Happy Humpback! "Humpback" is a description of how the whale arches its back out of the water when it gets ready to make a dive.

Diego knew he still had a long way to go to get to the humpback whale. He had to get over the sand dunes to reach the water. Time to call for Rescue Pack!

"You need a hot-air balloon!" said Rescue Pack, as he turned into one.

⑥ They made it to the water's edge, and Rescue Pack set Diego down on the ground.

Diego could see across the water to the rocky island where the baby humpback was stuck. He had to get to him. He looked into the water, but there were a lot of giant jellyfish!

"The jellyfish could sting us, but we've got to get to that whale!" he said. Diego looked in his Field Journal and saw that jellyfish are afraid of giant sea turtles.

"We can ride on the back of my friend Tuga the Leatherback Sea Turtle," he said. "She'll scare away the jellyfish."

Diego sat on top of Tuga as she began to swim across the water. The jellyfish soon disappeared!

FIELD JOURNAL ANIMAL FACTS
Whales, whales everywhere! Humpback whales are found in every ocean on Earth!

But then, Diego
spotted something else
in the water.

"Sharks!" said Diego.

Tuga swam as fast as
she could, escaping the
sharks. Soon, she got
to the rocky island
where the whale was.

"*Gracias,* Tuga," said Diego as he hopped off.
He waved good-bye as he ran down the sand to find
the whale.

"I'm stuck," said the
baby humpback when
Diego arrived.

"Don't worry," said
Diego. "I'm an Animal
Rescuer and I'll get you
back in the water."

"Thank you!" said
the whale.

Diego knew that a big wave was needed to move the whale back into the ocean. He called to the humpbacks, "*AOOO AHHH!*" Diego ran across the beach to meet them, and jumped on the back of one of the whales, so he could ride along.

"Splash, whales!" he called. When they splashed their tails, they moved the water

(8) enough to send the baby whale back to his mommy.

"*¡Gracias*, Diego!" called the baby humpback as he leaped out of the water.

"*¡Misión cumplida!* Rescue complete!" said Diego.

FIELD JOURNAL ANIMAL FACTS
Singers of the sea! All humpback whales can sing, but the male is the main singer of the family. The songs can be heard underwater!